Rover and Coo Coo

by John Hay

illustrated by Tim Solliday

A Star & Elephant Book
The Green Tiger Press
La Jolla
1986

To my mother and father with love.

Text and illustrations copyright © 1986 by The Green Tiger Press.
Library of Congress Catalog Card Number 86-81312
ISBN: 0-88138-078-4
Manufactured in Hong Kong.

Color separations by Photolitho AG, Gossau/Zurich, Switzerland.
The text is set in Century Schoolbook by
Commerce Graphics, San Diego, California.
Printed and bound by Colorcraft, Ltd., Hong Kong.

When I was a child, my father would tell me this story about my great-great-great-grandfather who lived in a wilderness in the early days when the Ohio River valley was a frontier. The story was never told to depict the usual habits of people or wolves, but is a story of nature in a broader sense. Customs and habits change and grow distant, leaving stories which are kept alive through the generations. They seem to have patterns to keep them always fresh. And storytelling is an ancient practice which can bring the gift of teaching.

Often my family will sit for hours together around the open fire or on the screen porch with the singing of the katydids and the crickets, to talk and laugh and hear stories such as this one, which is from a life on the American frontier.

John Hay
Kentucky
Summer 1986

Once a long time ago, in a real place, in a real log cabin, two great and powerful hounds, Rover and Coo Coo, lay sleeping before the fire. Mama Hay moved toward them quietly over the cabin floor, and as if by some instinct woven among their dreams, they sensed her and together rose to let her pass. While she knelt upon the hearth stones, they stood like ancient sentinels, watchful and protective, and at ease in the little cabin home. As Mama Hay stirred the warm broth in the pot among the embers, the two hounds towering beside her tilted their heads to the sounds of laughter that rippled through the open window.

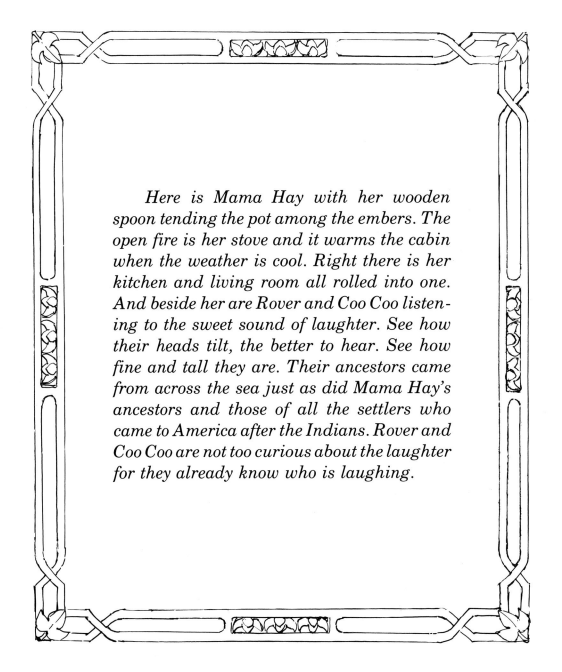

Here is Mama Hay with her wooden spoon tending the pot among the embers. The open fire is her stove and it warms the cabin when the weather is cool. Right there is her kitchen and living room all rolled into one. And beside her are Rover and Coo Coo listening to the sweet sound of laughter. See how their heads tilt, the better to hear. See how fine and tall they are. Their ancestors came from across the sea just as did Mama Hay's ancestors and those of all the settlers who came to America after the Indians. Rover and Coo Coo are not too curious about the laughter for they already know who is laughing.

Down by the little log building that held the corn that was picked from the field, Papa Hay was loading the yellow ears into sacks. He was a strong man, and his horse was strong for he took good care of her, and he wouldn't fill the sacks more than she could carry easily through the forest on the long, lonesome ride to the mill. Mama Hay had almost run out of meal to make their bread, so Papa Hay decided that if the day was sunny he would leave early for the mill so he could return home before nightfall. In the wilderness there were many dangers, but after nightfall there were even more. After dark the wolves hunt, the cougar roams, and robbers — men of little honor — find their chance.

We can find out much from a picture if we truly look. There is Papa Hay loading the yellow ears of corn into sacks. He is careful not to break too many kernels away from the cob that holds them. That is his horse, Spirit, beside him. He called her Spirit because she is so full of life, and because each time he spoke her name he was reminded of the force of creation on this beautiful earth. Behind him are his children playing tag. Dan has just slipped on a corn cob and Jenny has tagged him easily. They are laughing again because they are happy about almost everything. There in the cabin window we see Rover and Coo Coo. They are interested in the game of tag.

Papa Hay, whose real name was Charles, was young and handsome and strong. He enjoyed his work on the wilderness farm and enjoyed the times of quiet with his family. He liked to smile, and as he turned from securing the sacks from behind the saddle on Spirit's back, he gave a laugh and took off after Dan and Jenny. They ran away yelling; Rover and Coo Coo jumped out the window on the run, and Mama Hay went out the kitchen door in a wink, a frying pan in her hand.

"Hey," Mama Hay called out in perfect good cheer. "You all quit that skallydaggin' around."

At that, Charles scooped up both Dan and Jenny, one under each arm, as Rover and Coo Coo jumped and danced beside him. And suddenly Spirit, white as pure snow, came trotting up on her own.

"Can we go with you, Papa?" Dan asked, as Charles set them down by the cabin door.

"Yes, can we please?" Jenny added.

Rover and Coo Coco now stood calm and tall and watchful, for they sensed that their master would be traveling and were ready to go with him as well.

"Not today," Charles said. "I have a long ride through the forest and back. I want you all to stay here to take care of your mother."

And Mama Hay, young and beautiful, with auburn hair and yellow dress, stood by the cabin door, a soft smile at her lips, lightly holding the hem of her skirt, which she had just examined for a tear. And almost like dancing, with a turn of her slender shoulder, she glided to Charles, and on tiptoes, with her arms close around his neck, gave him a tender, loving kiss.

"Hurry back to us, my sweetheart," she whispered.

"As swift as the wind," he answered gently.

Charles, with his long rifle grasped firmly in one hand, swung into the saddle on Spirit's back. Rover and Coo Coo lunged forward to follow.

"Hold them," Charles said. "Or they will follow."

Mama Hay took the great dogs by the collar, one in each hand, and held them while Charles rode off into the dark forest. Once he turned to wave and the big dogs pulled against her, but she held them close and they knew well enough to mind. They all felt a moment of loneliness at Papa Hay's going, and Mama Hay had a small tear in the corner of one of her beautiful eyes. But just a small one.

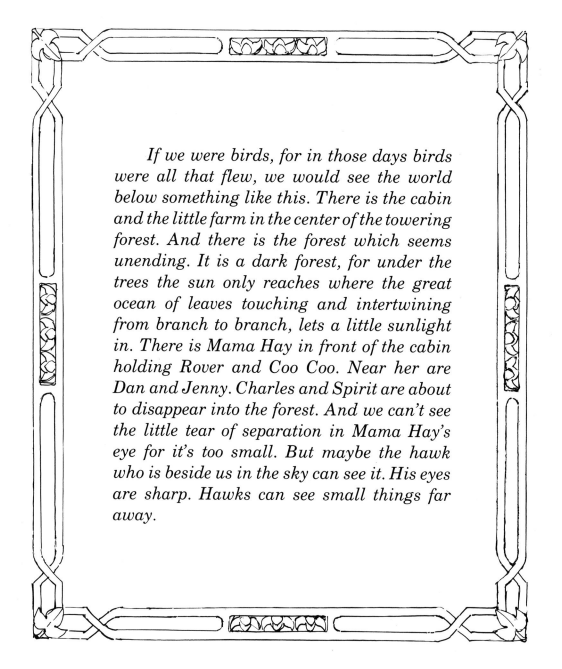

If we were birds, for in those days birds were all that flew, we would see the world below something like this. There is the cabin and the little farm in the center of the towering forest. And there is the forest which seems unending. It is a dark forest, for under the trees the sun only reaches where the great ocean of leaves touching and intertwining from branch to branch, lets a little sunlight in. There is Mama Hay in front of the cabin holding Rover and Coo Coo. Near her are Dan and Jenny. Charles and Spirit are about to disappear into the forest. And we can't see the little tear of separation in Mama Hay's eye for it's too small. But maybe the hawk who is beside us in the sky can see it. His eyes are sharp. Hawks can see small things far away.

The leaves were yellow and red and green for it was autumn, and as Charles urged Spirit into a gallop, the leaves which had fallen whirled and rustled under her feet. They made good speed as the trees seemed to sail by, and the wind, when it hit the leaves, would set them to falling like colorful rain, and Charles and Spirit rode on through the rain of leaves. They jumped the logs and the low bushes and galloped on. Spirit's mane lifted and shook and Charles' thick yellow hair lay out in the wind.

Suddenly seven deer burst across their path. They leapt and scattered and disappeared into the shadows of the forest. Charles thought about the shy deer, and then about the mill and how long it would take to get there, and about his home, and then about the wolves, and a shiver ran through him. He thought about his Indian friends who came in the spring and who didn't sleep in his cabin, but preferred to sleep out in the fresh air in his yard under the stars. He thought about robbers and how they roamed and ravaged and killed and had no concern but for themselves and the loot they could carry away. Even in the daylight hours he kept his eyes and ears sharp for them. He thought about the great strong dogs, Rover and Coo Coo, lying on the hearth before the fire, and about the bread that might be baking, and he felt hungry. But he rode on mightily with a warm red leaf caught in his hair.

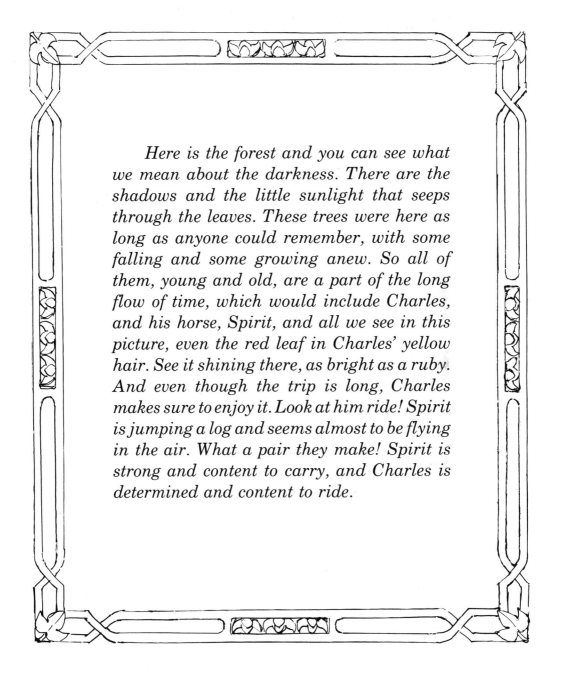

Here is the forest and you can see what we mean about the darkness. There are the shadows and the little sunlight that seeps through the leaves. These trees were here as long as anyone could remember, with some falling and some growing anew. So all of them, young and old, are a part of the long flow of time, which would include Charles, and his horse, Spirit, and all we see in this picture, even the red leaf in Charles' yellow hair. See it shining there, as bright as a ruby. And even though the trip is long, Charles makes sure to enjoy it. Look at him ride! Spirit is jumping a log and seems almost to be flying in the air. What a pair they make! Spirit is strong and content to carry, and Charles is determined and content to ride.

Hour after hour passed with time for rest and time for riding on, that balance which can make the world a pleasure. When at last they broke from the forest to the place where the mill was nestled right by a stream of fresh-flowing water at the foot of a craggy hill. What a sight it was! There were horse-drawn wagons and men on mules, carts and spotted horses. Whole families, who didn't live as far away from the mill as Charles, were packed into the back of spring wagons, and a group of children played together on the hillside. There, in the shade of a tree, was an Indian talking to an old man with a long, white, flowing beard. And the line of people waiting to have their grain ground at the mill was long. These were the people of the wilderness who had come from cabin homes scattered about the immense forest.

Charles rode up and took his place at the end of the long line, and though he saw a few people he knew, and chatted for awhile with each of them, the hours went by slowly and darkness was falling by the time his turn came to have his corn ground in the mill.

Beside the mill stood the Indian and the old man with the white beard. After Charles handed his sacks of corn to the miller, the old man spoke to him.

"You be Charles Hay, young man?"

"I am," Charles said.

"Well, I'm Jack Whitman and this be my friend, Three Feathers." Charles shook hands with Jack Whitman and nodded in a friendly manner to Three Feathers as was the Indian custom then.

"I heard you live through the forest to the north. My friend Three Feathers here says that wolves attacked an Indian boy and his pony in that forest. The boy escaped and the wolves killed the pony."

"I've heard of wolves attacking in past times," Charles said. "But I thought they had learned enough to be afraid of men. This is the first I've heard of such a thing."

"Maybe it's the hard winter of last year and the drought of the summer, for the game is scarce now and the wolves are surely hungry."

Jack Whitman and Three Feathers told Charles that it would be best if he waited until morning to travel the forest again. But Charles thought of his family at home and wanted to return to them, and he thought, "Maybe the wolves attacked the Indian boy and a pony, but they will never attack me."

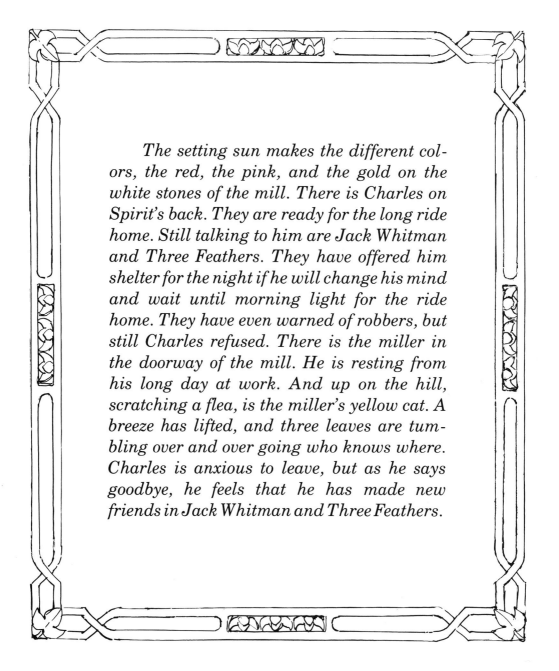

The setting sun makes the different colors, the red, the pink, and the gold on the white stones of the mill. There is Charles on Spirit's back. They are ready for the long ride home. Still talking to him are Jack Whitman and Three Feathers. They have offered him shelter for the night if he will change his mind and wait until morning light for the ride home. They have even warned of robbers, but still Charles refused. There is the miller in the doorway of the mill. He is resting from his long day at work. And up on the hill, scratching a flea, is the miller's yellow cat. A breeze has lifted, and three leaves are tumbling over and over going who knows where. Charles is anxious to leave, but as he says goodbye, he feels that he has made new friends in Jack Whitman and Three Feathers.

It was dark, dark as black leaves against the sky, dark as the moon behind a cloud, so dark that Charles allowed Spirit a loose rein for she knew the way and could find it better then he.

The clouds rolled over the rising moon so that the shadows of the forest seemed to jump and disappear and hold danger in their willowy arms. Then a lone wolf, deep in the forest ahead of them, began to howl, a howl that was at once lonely and beautiful, terrible and true. Spirit's ears went up, and Charles urged her into a faster gallop, riding low in the saddle. Another wolf answered the first, howling long and soft in the distance, and there was another answer, and another from far away. And Charles rode on through the forest toward the howling wolves and his cabin home.

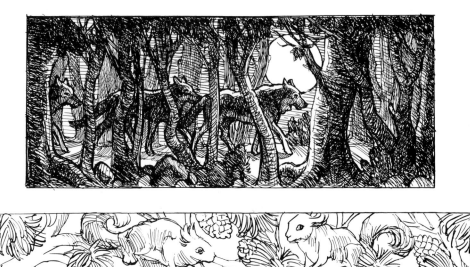

And then from out of nowhere a branch hanging low in the darkness caught against Charles' face and knocked him half out of the saddle. But he held on and felt the blood begin to run warm from a gash in his head. Soon the blood was in his eyes, and it was even difficult for him to watch the shadows of the trees. But he rode on low against Spirit's neck, on and on, and with every step he was closer to home and to the hunting wolves.

Charles felt an eerie silence in the forest. He knew that the howling of the wolves had come from this place. Spirit was weary and the steady rhythm of her hoofbeats seemed in the silence to tap against the great trees, and tap again. Charles wiped the blood from his eye and searched to either side in the dim light of the cloud-covered moon. He thought he saw a shadow slant in behind him and then another. He urged Spirit to go faster, and despite her weariness, she pushed ahead at a hard gallop, her ears up, sensing a presence in the forest.

Suddenly Spirit's legs slammed into a log among the shadows. She tried desperately to leap, but tumbled in the air, and Charles was thrown with a terrible force into the side of a tree and a bone in his arm snapped like a twig.

When horses fall, there is no telling what will happen. Often they tumble, often they slide, and often they roll, or in one fall may do all three. Sometimes they don't get up again. Their legs can break easily in a fall. A cat can fall and rarely be hurt, and a bear can tumble like a barrel and get right up. But there is not as much flexibility in a horse. And yet most often they get right up again too. There is Spirit turning like a pinwheel in the air. And there is Charles thrown like a shot against the tree. It looks as if he is stuck to the tree, hanging in an odd position. But the jolt that he felt was tremendous, and if you had been near, you could have heard the bone in his arm pop as it broke between the tree and the force of his body. If our picture were showing the few moments that follow, we would see Spirit and Charles lying in separate heaps on the forest floor. And there among the trees is a wolf frozen at the sight of the fall and waiting for his companions who are approaching swiftly on the trail.

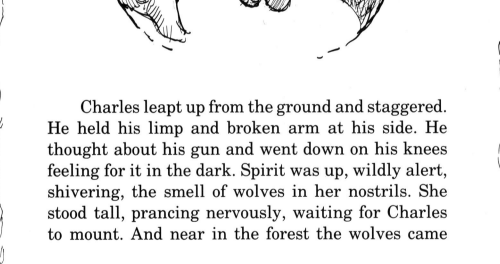

Charles leapt up from the ground and staggered. He held his limp and broken arm at his side. He thought about his gun and went down on his knees feeling for it in the dark. Spirit was up, wildly alert, shivering, the smell of wolves in her nostrils. She stood tall, prancing nervously, waiting for Charles to mount. And near in the forest the wolves came swiftly together, and the pack was on the scent. With blood in his eyes again, Charles gave up finding his gun, ran to Spirit's side, and with his good arm pulled himself into the saddle.

Spirit lurched into a gallop, and at the same moment a wolf was beside her in the air. The wolf sunk its teeth deep into Charles' leg with such force that its body twisted, its teeth pulled loose, and it flipped in midair to be left behind floundering in the golden leaves.

Three or four wolves — maybe more — began the chase after the tired and travel-worn horse and the wounded and bleeding rider. Charles was in great pain. His arm hung limp, his flesh was torn, but he was not a man to give up, and he was not a man who forgot to think. He thought of the two great hounds, Rover and Coo Coo, and that they might be able to save him, that maybe they would hear him and come. And so Charles raised his own voice, not unlike the howl of the wolf to his own kind, deep in some forest, Charles' call was at once lonely and beautiful, terrible and true, "Here...Rover...Here...Coo Coooo...seek...seeeek!"

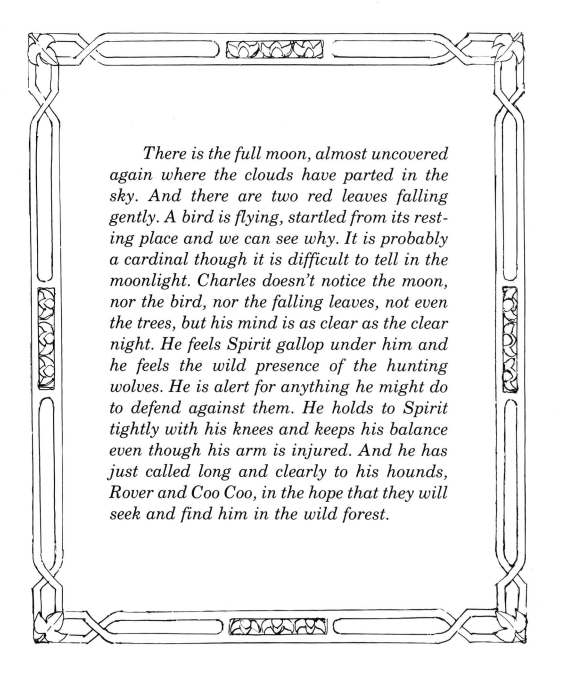

There is the full moon, almost uncovered again where the clouds have parted in the sky. And there are two red leaves falling gently. A bird is flying, startled from its resting place and we can see why. It is probably a cardinal though it is difficult to tell in the moonlight. Charles doesn't notice the moon, nor the bird, nor the falling leaves, not even the trees, but his mind is as clear as the clear night. He feels Spirit gallop under him and he feels the wild presence of the hunting wolves. He is alert for anything he might do to defend against them. He holds to Spirit tightly with his knees and keeps his balance even though his arm is injured. And he has just called long and clearly to his hounds, Rover and Coo Coo, in the hope that they will seek and find him in the wild forest.

And hearing the sound of their master's voice traveling to them through the forest, Rover and Coo Coo stood up at once in the cabin and began to scratch at the door. Mama Hay, who could not hear the voice calling, ignored them, thinking they heard only some animal in the yard that they wished to chase. She looked up once at the dogs, then went back to her reading while the children played quietly on the floor with a small house of sticks.

Spirit slowed her step to jump a dead tree, and as she leapt, a wolf lunged and sunk his teeth into her shoulder. Its huge body hung for moments against Charles' leg, and its growl roared in the night air. Charles reined Spirit to one side against a tree so that the wolf that held her with its teeth was knocked away. Charles urged Spirit on, and she ran with all that was left in her while the wolves snarled and slashed behind, leaving deep wounds that ran with blood. Riding blindly, Charles lifted his voice again and the words came out, a desperate and ancient song, his call for help, "Here...Rover...Coo Coooo...seeek...seeeek!"

In the cabin the air was charged. Rover and Coo Coo clawed wildly against the door and jumped and barked and went to their mistress and pushed at her with their noses; their huge bodies were taut and seemed to fill the room. The children, frightened, stood frozen in wonder while the long, soft call which only the dogs could hear rose again in the air, "Here...Rover...Coo Cooo...seeek...seeeek!" Rover's and Coo Coo's eyes filled with wildness as they stood on their hind legs against the door and howled their answer.

Suddenly Mama Hay felt a message in her own heart, and had a great yearning toward her absent husband, and knew in the core of the moment that she must take a chance and turn the dogs free. Out the door, they were gone to the shadows like pieces of gray light.

A dog has a different kind of ear and can hear sounds that we will miss. Rover and Coo Coo heard and understood the need. We see Rover by the door trying desperately for a way out, and there is Coo Coo nudging at Mama Hay with her nose, trying to let her know that she must set them free. There are Dan and Jenny standing back. They have knocked over the little house of sticks. Suddenly Mama Hay senses what Rover and Coo Coo already know. We see her look toward the door, knowing that she must open it. We can see that Dan and Jenny are watchful and want to discover why Rover and Coo Coo are acting in a way they have never seen before. They feel the strange excitement of the dogs and sense some kind of danger. Maybe later they will think this over and wonder what sort of messages the dogs were able to hear in Charles' voice.

Spirit ran with all her heart and Charles held on with his one good hand. But Spirit, tiring with each heavy breath, made Charles wonder if she would be able to go on. The wolves that had felt the sting of her kick were loping behind, until all in one instant they made another dash to pull the horse and rider down. As the blood ran again into Charles' eyes and blinded him, and as the first wolf hit Spirit in the flank and made a bloody slash, Rover and Coo Coo came pounding in through the undergrowth and charged into the pack of wolves, howling and deadly.

Spirit and Charles galloped on and not a wolf followed; again they felt the peace of the wilderness. Through the dark trees Charles could hear the sounds of the terrible fighting until the sounds grew dim, and he galloped out of the silent forest into the yard of his cabin home. There, the only sound was a little owl hoohooing his song. Mama Hay saw Charles from the window and ran out to help him down from Spirit's back. Without a word she held him in her arms, and Charles felt his pains begin to ease.

The hooing of the little owl trickled through the night, cool and tender. In the cabin Charles sat near the crackling fire with Mama Hay, Jenny and Dan. They had dressed his wounds and bandaged him and

had found a little hickory stick to make a splint for his broken arm so that it would heal. They also tended to Spirit's wounds and gave her plenty of fresh water and grassy hay. Only Rover and Coo Coo were still missing from the family gathering. Charles left the front door open just a crack so that if they returned they could push it with their paws or their noses and come in. The night wind made a little bit of a moan through the crack at the door, but no Rover and Coo Coo came to push it open.

"Will we ever see Rover and Coo Coo?" Jenny asked as she put up her hand to wipe away a tear.

"We hope so," Charles said in a comforting voice. "They are very strong."

"I think I hate wolves," Dan said. "Don't you hate them, Daddy?"

"No, I don't hate wolves," Charles said.

"But they hurt you."

"A wolf is a creature with a place in nature. Why be mad at a wolf, Dan? He is following the only way he knows."

"So why doesn't he learn better?" Dan asked.

"Maybe he will in his own way. Some say the wolf learned early to avoid men. So though we must be watchful, we can accept the wolf and try to understand his ways.

"I'm not sure," Dan said.

"And I'm not either," said little Jenny as she leaned against her mother for comfort.

"Every creature and every thing has a song," Mama Hay said as she took little Jenny into her arms. "Each has a song and that song is its own. A rock has a song, the wolf has a song, Rover and Coo Coo have a song, and the little owl in the tree is singing part of his tonight, hear it." They all sat very still and listened to the sweet singing of the owl. "That song is their nature within. Even we have our special song. And as people, we could make it the sweetest of all."

Everyone was quiet, for Mama Hay's words, and her feeling, and her heart, all that beauty, seemed to fill the room with love. And just then, a paw pushed the cabin door open, and Rover and Coo Coo stepped in. They went to each member of the family with their silent greeting, but slowly for they were weary and wounded. They had done what was in them to do and had come again to take their place in the home. Mama Hay gave them water, and Charles tended their wounds while Dan and Jenny petted their heads to comfort them. Mightily they had protected the family and mightily they would again, and that night they rested another time on the warm stones of the hearth.

Here we have six pictures, but that's not a lot. The first is of Rover and Coo Coo standing in the sun in summer. They are watchful and content. The second is a lone wolf on a rock on a hill at nightfall. Soon he will be hunting. And the next is of Spirit at sunrise listening to the neighing of another horse. The fourth is of the little owl in the tree calling to its mate. The fifth picture is of the moon and the tree and the rock and the grass and the wind. You can't see the wind, but you know it is there. The last picture, the biggest one of all, is of the family at the moment when Mama Hay spoke softly of the way the world is made. She knew that they all fit with the owl and the wolf and the grass and the horse and the wind. That's why six pictures are not a lot, for in the world there is so much we could draw — and so much, like the wind, we couldn't draw. And the world is one picture, and the family is there together, learning the notes of their song.

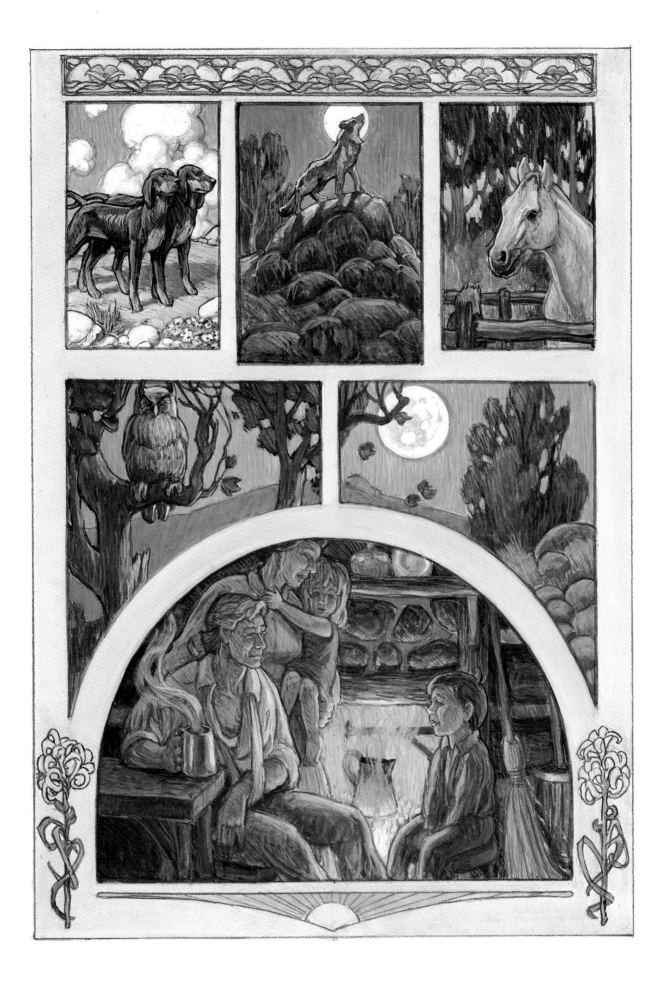